Hip-Dip-Dip
with
Mouse
Mole

Joyce Dunbar

Illustrated by Alison de Vere

CORGI PUPS

Series Reading Consultant: Prue Goodwin
Reading and Language Information Centre,
University of Reading

HIP-DIP-DIP WITH MOUSE AND MOLE
A CORGI PUPS BOOK : 0 552 546739

First publication in Great Britain

PRINTING HISTORY
Corgi Pups edition published 2000

1 3 5 7 9 10 8 6 4 2

Set in 18/25pt Bembo Schoolbook by
Phoenix Typesetting, Ilkley, West Yorkshire

Corgi Pups Books are published by Transworld Publishers,
61-63 Uxbridge Road, London W5 5SA,
a division of The Random House Group Ltd,
in Australia by Random House Australia (Pty) Ltd,
20 Alfred Street, Milsons Point, Sydney, NSW 2061, Australia,
in New Zealand by Random House New Zealand Ltd,
18 Poland Road, Glenfield, Auckland 10, New Zealand
and in South Africa by Random House (Pty) Ltd,
Endulini, 5a Jubilee Road, Parktown 2193, South Africa

Made and printed in Great Britain by
Cox & Wyman Ltd, Reading, Berkshire

Contents

Hip–Dip–Dip   5

A Frisky Fluttery Ghost   24

Atishoo!   44

Hip-Dip-Dip

There was a toy boat in Hare's shop window; a blue boat with a white sail.

"Look at that boat," said Mole. "It's just what I've always wanted."

"Is it?" said Mouse.

"It is," said Mole.

"Then why don't you buy it?"
said Mouse.

"I don't have enough money
saved up," said Mole.

"I've got enough money," said Mouse. "Why don't I buy it for you?"

"Will you, Mouse? Will you really? It isn't my birthday, you know."

"But it will be, one of these days," said Mouse.

"So it will," smiled Mole.

They went home for Mouse
to get his money. Mole was so
excited. He skipped and jumped
all the way.

"Hip-dip-dip
My blue ship
Sailing on the water
Like a cup and saucer
You . . . are . . . *it*!"

he sang gaily.

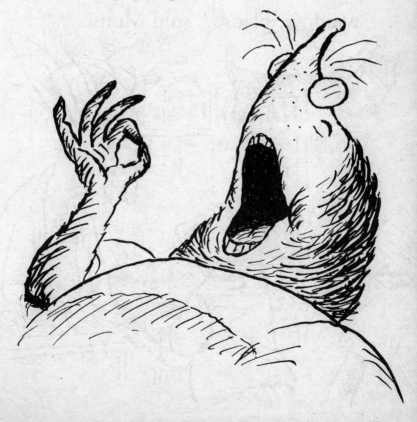

Mouse emptied
his money sock.
He had just
enough saved up.
They soon arrived
back at the shop.

"The blue boat in the
window, please," said Mouse.

Hare took the boat from the window and placed it on the counter. "There you are," she said; "a blue boat with a white sail."

Mouse was about to hand over his money when Mole gave a little squawk. "Look, Mouse.

There's another boat on the
shelf, a red one with a green
sail."

"So there is," said Mouse.

"I think I like that one better,"
said Mole.

Hare took the red boat with the green sail and put it on the counter next to the blue boat with the white sail. "There you are," she said. "Take your pick."

Mole looked from one to the other. "I can't make up my mind, Mouse," he said.

"I've got others if you'd like to see them," said Hare, reaching under the counter. "See, here's a yellow boat with a striped sail."

"Oh dear," said Mole, picking up each boat in turn, "I don't know which one I like best."

"How about this orange one with a black sail?" said Hare, putting it side by side with the others.

"This is all too much," wailed Mole. "Now I'll *never* be able to make up my mind," and he stumbled blindly out of the shop and down the road.

That night Mole had many-
coloured dreams. He was very
bleary-eyed the next morning.

"Have you made up your
mind?" asked Mouse.

"No," said Mole, "I haven't."

"Can't you just do 'Hip-dip-
dip . . . my blue ship' and choose
that way?" said Mouse.

"I've been doing it all night,"
sighed Mole. "My blue ship. My
red ship. My yellow ship. And I
still can't make up my mind!"

"It's a perfect day for sailing boats on the pond," said Mouse.

"I *know*!" moaned Mole.

"Why don't we go back to the shop and have another look?" said Mouse.

But when they arrived at Hare's, they found there were only three boats.

"Where's the blue boat?"
asked Mole.

"I'm sorry, it went this
morning," said Hare.

"It didn't! It can't have!"
protested Mole.

"It did," said Hare, "to a
mystery buyer on the
telephone."

"But the blue boat is the one I really wanted!" said Mole. "It's the one I liked best of all!"

"Are you sure about that?" asked Mouse.

"Sure as sure!" said Mole.

"Good," said Mouse, "because . . .

I am the mystery buyer."

"Oh, Mouse!" said Mole.

"Oh, Mole," said Mouse.

"But where is it?" asked Mole.

"Waiting for us under the counter," said Mouse. "We could take it on the pond right now."

Mole tucked the boat under his arm. "How lucky I am to have a mystery Mouse for a friend," he said. "I think we should share this boat. After me, you can have first go."

And off they went, singing,

"Hip-dip-dip
My blue ship
Sailing on the water
Like a cup and saucer
We . . . are . . . *it*!"

A Frisky Fluttery Ghost

It was a bright and breezy morning. Mouse opened the window and took a deep breath of air. "We can have breakfast outside in the garden today," he said to himself. "Mole will like that."

Mole was still snoring in bed.

Mouse got the breakfast ready on a tray. He made a pile of crispy buttery toast. "Mole!" he called. "Breakfast!"

Mole didn't appear.

"Mole!" called Mouse a few
moments later. "You're missing a
beautiful morning."

Mouse hung out some
washing while he was waiting.
Still no sign of Mole.

Mouse nibbled a crust of
toast. "If I wait much longer for
Mole," he sighed, "I shall miss
the morning too. Mole!" he
called. "Your breakfast is waiting
for you. Crispy buttery toast."

Mole's head was under the
bedclothes. "What?" he called. "I
can't hear you."

"There's some crispy buttery toast waiting for you!" Mouse mumbled with his mouth full.

"*What?*" said Mole. "There's a *frisky fluttery ghost* waiting for me? Don't be silly, Mouse."

Mole peered blearily out of the window. He saw the washing, fluttering on the line.

The washing waved cheerily at Mole. He dived straight back under the bedclothes. "Ooohhh! There *is* a frisky fluttery ghost waiting for me! I'm staying in bed!"

Mouse finished hanging out
the washing. He nibbled another
crust of toast. He gave some
crumbs to the birds.

"Mole really is too bad," he
said to himself. "I'll go and give
him a good shake."

Mole was a hump on the bed.
"Lazybones!" said Mouse,
pulling off the blankets.

"Don't hurt me!" squealed
Mole.

"What's the matter, Mole?"
said Mouse, tugging at the sheet.
"Come on! Get up!"

"No I never!" squealed Mole. "Go away, frisky fluttery ghost!"

Mouse gave the hump a good shake. "Wake up, Mole! Wake up! You're having a bad dream."

"Ow!" squeaked Mole. "Please leave me alone."

"Whatever is the matter?" said Mouse.

Mole blinked in the sunlight. "Mouse! It's you! Thank goodness! Has it gone? Have you scared it away?"

"What?" asked Mouse.

"The frisky fluttery ghost!"

"I don't know what you're
talking about," said Mouse. "It's
a bright and breezy morning
and I have hung out the
washing and made some crispy
buttery toast. But I didn't see a
frisky fluttery ghost."

"*I* did," said Mole. "It came in
through the window and shook
me! Look out! It might be just
behind you!"

But Mouse was too frightened
to look. He dived straight under
the bedclothes with Mole.

They huddled together for a
good long while.

"Do you think it's gone yet?"
said Mole. "I'm hungry."

"I think it must have," said
Mouse. "I think we can get out
now."

"Let's roar and growl," said
Mole. "If we sound fierce
enough, that will scare away
any ghost."

So, roaring and growling as
loudly as they could, Mouse and
Mole crept downstairs.

"There you are, see, it's gone!"
said Mouse.

"So it has!" said Mole.

They made a big pot of tea
and some fresh crispy buttery
toast.

"It's too late for breakfast,"
said Mouse. "Let's call it lunch
instead."

And they did.

It was such a pity it started to
rain.

"Quick! Let's get the washing
in!" said Mouse.

Mole grabbed hold of a sheet.
"Washing? What washing?"
he said. "I think the ghosts are
getting wet! Ooooooooh!
Hoooooooowl! Whooooh!"

Atishoo!

"Atishoo!" went Mouse.

"Bless you," said Mole.

"Atishoo!" went Mouse again.

"Have you got a cold, Mouse?" asked Mole. "Are you feeling ill?"

"Atishoo!" went Mouse.

"But Mouse, you *never* catch cold. You are *never* ill."

"A-a-a-tishoo!" went Mouse.

"I think you *do* have a cold. I think you *are* ill," said Mole. "You have a red nose. Your eyes look very watery. Your fur looks out of sorts."

"A-a-a-a-tishoo!" went
Mouse.

"Never mind, Mouse. I will
take good care of you. I'll
mollycoddle you. How would
you like to be mollycoddled?"

"A-a-a-atishoo!" went
Mouse.

"How about breakfast-in-
bed-with-first-look-at-today's-
comic-followed-by-a-nice-
warm-bath?"

"A-a-a-a-atishoo!" went
Mouse.

"Good," said Mole. "I
thought you'd like that."

Mole went to the bathroom
and started to run the bath.

Then he went to the kitchen and
started to make breakfast. He
made hot buttered toast fingers –
just the way *he* liked them. He
boiled an egg – just the way *he*

liked it. He took the marmalade
from the cupboard – just the sort
he liked. He made peppermint
tea – *his* favourite. Then he put
them all on a tray.

"That looks wonderful!" he sighed and set off upstairs to see Mouse.

But then he had a thought. "What a thoughtless Mole I am," he said to himself. "This breakfast is all just right for me, but it may not be right for Mouse. I shall have to try it, just to make sure."

Mole sat down at the bottom of the stairs to make sure.

"Delicious!" he said when he had eaten the boiled egg with toast fingers.

"Scrumptious," he said when he had polished off the marmalade.

"Perfect," he said, sipping down the peppermint tea.

"A-a-a-a-tishoo!" went
Mouse from upstairs.

"Dearie me," said Mole,
wiping his snout. "Never mind,
the comic has just arrived. I'll
just have a little look through to
make sure it will cheer Mouse
up."

"Tee-hee," chortled Mole as he sat at the bottom of the stairs with the comic.

"A-a-a-atishoo!" went Mouse from upstairs.

Mole crumpled up the comic in a panic. "Mouse's bath!" he yelled. "I've forgotten Mouse's bath!"

He dashed into the bathroom
and turned off the taps. The bath
was filled to the brim. The
bubbles were scented and
shining. The steam rose through
the air.

"I hope it's warm enough for Mouse," said Mole. "I'll try it, just to be sure. And while I'm at it I may as well finish the comic."

So Mole had a good long soak and read the comic from cover to cover. The comic got soggier and soggier while the water got colder and colder. But Mole didn't notice. He chuckled and chortled away. "What a good comic this is," he said.

"This will make Mouse feel
better."

By the time Mole had finished, the comic was too soggy to read and the water had gone stone cold. Mole's teeth began to chatter. His shivering made his fur stand on end. He wrapped himself in a towel and went plodding off to see Mouse.

"Mouse," said Mole, "I made you breakfast and had to try it to make sure it was perfect. It was. I checked the comic to make sure it was funny. It was. I tested the bath water to make sure it was warm. It was, but it isn't any longer. The water has gone stone cold. I'm cold too.

Look at me, Mouse, I'm sh-sh-
shivering to the t-t-t-tip of my
s-s-s-snout! I shall have to go to
bed to get warm. But look, I
brought you the comic. I hope it
makes you feel better. Mouse, I
shall need someone to mollycoddle me."

"Atishoo!" went Mouse.
"Atishoo! Atishoo! Atishoo!"
went Mole.

THE END

Don't miss the next stories
about Mouse and Mole...

The Ups and Downs of
Mouse and Mole

Coming soon from
Corgi Pups